MW00763727

DR. TENTH
Christmas Surprise!

originated by Roger Hargreaves

Written and illustrated by Adam Hargreaves

Manufactured in China.

ISBN 9781524786236   10 9 8 7 6 5 4 3 2

It was Christmas Eve. The Doctor sat in front of a crackling fire and wished that he could light a real one.

But the TARDIS did not have a chimney.

He sipped a mug of hot chocolate.

And Donna sipped hers.

"Hot chocolate is my favorite thing in the world," announced Donna. "I hope I get a surprise for Christmas."

"You will have to wait and see," said the Doctor. "Now, what we need is a Christmas tree. We might not have a real fire, but we are going to have a real Christmas tree."

He got up to go out.

"But I haven't finished my hot chocolate," said Donna.

"Have it later," said the Doctor.

"But it will get cold," she replied.

"Then bring it with you."

The Doctor and Donna set off to town.

There was no traffic on the roads, because of the heavy snow, but there were lots of snowmen.

"Somebody has been busy," said Donna.

"You're right," agreed the Doctor. "But I'm not sure who made them. They don't look like very friendly snowmen."

And as it happened, they were not friendly at all.

In fact, they were rather scary snowmen.

Rather scary snowmen who suddenly started chasing the Doctor and Donna down the street!

Suddenly the street was deserted, and looking over his shoulder, the Doctor realized that Donna and the snowmen had disappeared.

The snowmen had captured Donna!

"Ho! Ho! Ho!" laughed a voice behind the Doctor.

He spun around to find himself face-to-face with Santa Claus.

"Ho! Ho! Ho!"

But this was not a jolly, fun "Ho! Ho! Ho!" This was a nasty, unpleasant, metallic-sounding "Ho! Ho! Ho!"

This was not the real Santa.

The Doctor drew out his sonic screwdriver and took control of the robotic imposter.

"Take me to the snowmen," he demanded.

The Santa robot led the Doctor a little way out of town, where they came to a large igloo.

The Doctor disabled the Santa-bot and crept inside the igloo.

At first sight, it seemed a very festive scene.

The room was filled with snowmen and Santa Clauses.

And there was a Christmas tree in the corner.

But it was far from festive.

In the middle of the gathering was Donna,
tied up with tinsel.

And still holding her mug of hot chocolate.

Looking around the igloo, the Doctor saw what he needed.

Using his sonic screwdriver, he activated a string of Christmas lights, which wound themselves around and around the snowmen and the Santa-bots.

The Doctor and Donna made their escape on a sled.

But the Doctor had forgotten the Christmas tree.

A Christmas tree that was, of course, no ordinary Christmas tree.

It came racing down the slope in pursuit of them, firing Christmas ornaments as it went.

"This is not the sort of Christmas surprise I had in mind!" cried Donna.

The sled took a direct hit and was tipped over.

The Doctor and Donna were sent sprawling in the snow.

"Quickly!" cried Donna. "Use your sonic screwdriver to disable the tree!"

But the Doctor had lost it in the snow.

Donna looked at her mug of hot chocolate.

It was no longer hot.

"Yuck!" she exclaimed, and threw it over the advancing tree.

The liquid short-circuited the tree's wiring, and with a fizz and a puff of smoke, it came to a standstill.

"Ho, ho, ho," chuckled a voice behind them.

"Oh no!" cried the Doctor. "It's another Santa-bot!"

With no weapons left, the Doctor and Donna pelted the Santa Claus with snowballs.

"Stop, stop!" cried the Santa Claus. "I'm the real Santa!"

And indeed, he was.

"I'm so sorry," apologized the Doctor. "I hope this doesn't put us on your naughty list."

"Ho, ho, ho," chuckled Santa, brushing the snow off. "No harm done, but I must be on my way. Lots to do!"

The Doctor and Donna carried the Christmas tree back to the TARDIS.

The next day, Christmas Day, the Doctor and Donna opened their stockings.

"Well, at least Santa didn't put us on his naughty list," said the Doctor. "Look, he has given me a new sonic screwdriver!"

"And here is the Christmas surprise I was looking for. He has given me a hot-chocolate machine!" cried Donna.

"What you might call a . . ."

". . . hot-choc-bot!" laughed the Doctor.
"Ho! Ho! Ho!"